Cherry Blossom And Other Stories

AMY LAURENS

OTHER WORKS

Find more about the author:
www.AmyLaurens.com

CHERRY BLOSSOM AND OTHER STORIES

AMY LAURENS

AUSTRALIA

Paperback ISBN: 978-1-923305-06-9
eBook ISBN: 9781502228185

www.inkprintpress.com

National Library of Australia Cataloguing-in-Publication Data
Laurens, Amy 1985—
Cherry Blossom And Other Stories
96 p.   cm.
ISBN: 978-1-923305-06-9
Inkprint Press, Canberra, Australia
1. Fiction—Fantasy—Collections & Anthologies 2. Fiction—Fantasy—Contemporary 3. Poetry—Women Authors

Summary: A collection of spellbinding short tales and poetry brimming with quiet magic, haunting transformations, and what it means to be female in relationships.

Second Edition: February 2026
Cover design © Inkprint Press
Cover image © olgaboykophoto via Deposit Photos

CONTENTS

For Glam, my guide.

INTRODUCTION

THE INTERACTION BETWEEN OURSELVES AND OUR ART IS A fascinating one on many levels, but something that's particularly fascinated me more and more the longer I spend in creative spaces is the way that we experience our own voice.

...No, there's no need to be so highbrow about this. Let me put it plainly:

For a long while, this book was out of print because I thought it sucked.

Not the individual stories and poems per se, but the whole, the collection. I thought it felt random and incoherent as a collection, with too disparate genres and forms for it to be successful. But that was because I was a beginner who couldn't see my own voice, couldn't see that what I took for imperfections were simply deviations from the norm—which is often all imperfections are, really—and that it was these very deviations that made the book *mine*.

Rereading it years later, I was struck by the similarity in all these works: not in their genre or form, but in their tone, their thematic approaches, their essence. This collection is as accurate a snapshot as it's possible to have of me at that time in my life; it reflects the ideas I found important enough to write about, the experiences that were bubbling away in my subconscious, the things I cared about—and yes, even the vocabulary I preferred and how I expressed myself.

Brandon Sanderson once said that every book you write, every piece of art you create, is perfect, because it's a perfect expression of who you are at the moment.

And so it's with appreciation for the me who existed in the late twenty-aughts and very early twenty-teens that I have brought this book back to the world. That younger, anxious, more brittle self—along with all the thousand variations that have existed before and since —made me who I am today, and I can't but love her for that.

And so, I hope you enjoy this moody, emotional collection of works about human relationships and how we find who we are in the context of them, full of shadows and subconscious motivations that gradually break free to something dawningly innocent, something wholesome in its desire to be nothing more or less than ourself, whole.

I have so much compassion for the me who wrote this book; I hope you find something in her to love as well.

Amy

CHERRY BLOSSOM

AMBROSE SITS ALONE IN UTTER DARKNESS, NO ONE BUT FEAR for company as he prepares for the culmination of his ambitions. It's been years since he felt fear; it's been years since he felt anything. That was one of the demands of the quest: let nothing distract him from his single-mindedness, not love, not hatred, not regret, not fear. So in a way, it's nice to feel again, even if it does set his teeth on edge and send his pulse racing.

There's no reason for the fear, of course. He knows the potion will work. Years of research and millions of dollars have ensured that. But the moisture that should coat his tongue and throat still slicks his palms and forehead instead. Ambrose scrubs his hands on his bare thighs; his grip must be firm, sure. The timing of this experiment is so crucial to its success; the merest half-millisecond hesitation caused by a slip of the knife would be disastrous—and he doesn't want to die.

Which is entirely the point, really. He sits here, naked and alone, in the dark of night in a house nobody wanted on a rug nobody loved, because he is about to reach the pinnacle of his ambitions, and finally, at last, escape the clutches of death forever.

Shame he has to die to do it.

Ambrose takes a deep breath and feels for the knife to his right and the stone goblet to his left. Careful not to spill the precious liquid, he raises the goblet to his lips, fingers wrapped around stone so smooth it feels wet. Or is that sweat again? In his other hand he clutches the knife, simple wooden hilt roughing his skin, and presses the blade to his throat. It's cold and somehow it tickles.

Fear leaps in his stomach but he catches it, moulds it, hones it until it's as sharp as the blade and is just another weapon at his disposal. He tilts the goblet until the liquid meets his lips, presses the blade into his skin until he feels the sting of blood. This is it, the moment when he will end his life and begin it, the moment when he will grasp his immortality. On the silent count of three, he draws the knife across his throat and swallows down the potion.

Hot fire grips him, and whether from the wound or liquid, he can't tell, and it doesn't matter, because the pain sears down into his belly and he can't breathe, can't scream, and his heart stutters.

He's dying.

His muscles cramp, arching his spine until he knows his bones must shatter from the strain, and it burns, flames under his skin that light him up like a candle.

The fear bursts from his grip and floods through him on a tide of adrenalin. Everything's done, everything's over, and it was all for nothing, and the only thing he can think of is Lena's eyes and a spray of cherry blossom in the moonlight. In despair that overwhelms even the pain, he passes out.

When he wakes, the fire has died down, and only the embers are left. They flare in his joints and limbs when he stirs, and at first he is too groggy to realise what they mean.

Ambrose strains open his eyes and stares vaguely at a stone goblet lying on its side, rim chipped, the sticky residue of black, tar-like liquid pooling underneath it.

The memories flood back and he wonders how long it's been. Will Morris have missed him yet?

He struggles to his feet, biting back moans as his muscles catch and clench—but then he grins. He's standing. He died, and now he's standing, and he feels...

Ambrose stretches and twists, staring at his body, wondering exactly what it is he feels. He's happy that it worked, of course; he's achieved the ambition of several lifetimes, and beaten all the others who raced against him. But it's a quiet sort of happiness, reserved, not at all the elation he'd expected. And underneath it all, he realises, there's still the stink of fear. What if they don't believe him?

Suddenly frantic, Ambrose strides to the corner of the room and his bundle of clothes. He dresses, not worrying over minor things like buttons, and hurries from the room.

Downstairs, out in front, his car is waiting and in it is his phone, left there so he wouldn't be disturbed. He punches in the speed dial for the office and fidgets as it rings. Morris will know; his elder brother always understands.

The secretary—Sarah? Sara?—answers the phone and Ambrose snaps for Morris. An awkward silence fills the end of the line. His stomach sinks. "What? What is it?" he demands.

"He's dead, Ambrose," the secretary says. "They found him in his flat three days ago. Suicide. We... He had no idea where you'd gone, Ambrose. He thought you'd left us."

Ambrose leans back as the world reels around him. "Three days? How long have I been gone?"

"A week."

Numb, Ambrose hangs up. He's achieved immortality, only it doesn't matter, because he was going to share it with Morris. Not that he'd ever told Morris that, not in so many words, but the promise was there, implied. And now it's too late.

It's a month later, and still the mobs haven't died away. They never use the doorbell, just lie in wait around the front of the old, unloved house that's now his refuge, waiting for him to appear. When he does, it's all flashing lights and questions, microphones in his face. He's tried his best to ignore them, but they're persistent, and they want to know his secrets. It's enough to make him wish he'd never publicised his findings, never made it known that he'd finally won.

Even at night they wolf around the steps, and it's hard for him to spot them because the moon has disappeared.

To be sure, the moon has always been sporadic. Despite rumours that centuries ago the moon was constant in its cycle, in all of living history it's been inconstant, full one night and new the next. But never has it been gone so long.

Morris is gone, the moon is gone, and even Lena, the lovesick, moony-eyed girl that used to follow him everywhere, is gone, and he feels utterly alone.

Outside, the mobs catch sight of his shadow through the frosted panes of the door and begin their restless murmurs. He needs food, needs to walk—but he can't face the mob again, not alone.

He leans his forehead on the ice-cold glass in the door. He's got everything he ever wanted, but no one told him the emptiness would feel like this. Even though he can remember the taste of Lena's lips that night under the last full moon, even though he can remember losing his focus for a split second in the pleasure of holding another warm body, of her skin pressing against his in the moonlight—it's not enough.

She'd tried, of course. All she wanted was to be with him, to love him. But immortality was a harsh master and he couldn't afford an entanglement, a distraction from his research. All he'd wanted was some fun on the side.

Only now she's gone, and he's standing here, barricaded in his own house by mobs of reporters and spies and conspirators, and he can't leave, can't go outside, and all he can see is the pain and confusion in her eyes as he'd turned and stridden away.

He'd never meant to hurt her.

The whirr of something moving quickly through the air cuts into his memories and he jerks away from the door. Where his head had rested only instants ago, the glass now sprouts a crossbow bolt that fizzes and sizzles.

Ambrose laughs, which turns into a sob. He's immortal, don't they understand? But it's obvious that they won't stop trying. He reaches out and bolts the deadlock. He'll order in groceries, find some way around it. Either way, he won't set foot outside again.

It's an ordinary night when Ambrose pelts down the hallway to answer the bell, sprinting so he doesn't have a chance to change his mind. For the last month without fail, someone has left cherry blossoms on his doorstep, and he knows it's Lena.

She told him once—or maybe twice—that cherry blossoms were her favourite, that they reminded her of everything good in life and how fragile and ephemeral it all was. And no one else has ever rung the bell.

The reporters left not long after he swore himself to hermitism, and the snoops and gold-diggers followed a few months later. The assassins took the longest to give up, but it's been at least a year now since the last attempt, so he feels confident flinging the door wide open and peering left and right, hoping for any glimpse of Lena.

As always, he's greeted by an empty street—only tonight is not so ordinary after all. It takes a moment for him to realise what's wrong, what's different, and when he does, he falls back a step, eyes wide: the moon is shining.

He'd always had the sneaking suspicion that it was because he'd died that the moon had gone, but here, hanging above the darkly silhouetted trees, is proof that he was wrong. A quiet sort of relief fills him; it wasn't his fault after all.

Feeling as close to cheerful as it's possible to get when you gave up on feelings a decade ago, Ambrose leans down to retrieve the spray of blossom, and a thrill runs through him. The blossom is there, of course, pale pink petals drenched in silver light, the branch a sharp shadow beneath—but there is more. Tonight, the spray rests on a stack of letters, envelopes hand-folded from thick cream paper and addressed in fluid, loopy writing that's Lena all over.

His pulse skips as he snatches them up and carries them inside.

Why letters? he thinks. Why now? For a month she'd come to visit every night, and for a month he'd been too anxious to answer the door until she'd gone. Is she giving up?

He doesn't know how he feels about that, and he stares at the bundle apprehensively. On the one hand, he never professed to love her; never bought her roses, never sent her chocolates, never wrote her cards on Valentine's Day or birthdays. She'd been a bit of fun, a bluebell in the middle of an icy winter, and nothing more.

But on the other hand, she'd been sweet, and innocent, and every bloody thing he'd let go for immortality.

And she'd followed him past death, the only person from his former life to make an effort, to pound against the wall he'd built around himself.

Ambrose sits down in the armchair and pulls at the silky pink ribbon that holds the bundle together. It comes away, spilling cherry petals in his lap. He lifts what remains of the spray, feeling somehow responsible for the flowers' death.

Which is stupid, of course. Lena is the one who picked them, who killed them, and if she intended for him to keep them she should have brought something more robust, like chrysanthemums or lilies or sunflowers. She always was impractical.

He sets the branch aside, conscience prickling as he tries to avoid comparing Lena to a cherry flower, wondering if something might make her wither, and if that something might have been him.

Morris had always said that it was selfish to lead her on, to dance when he never meant to stay.

Ambrose cracks the seal on the first letter and unfolds it. He stares at it for a moment before realising that it details their first encounter, and a phrase catches his eye:

Why the Fates have chosen you as my target, I cannot untangle. But if you need me, I will persist as long as they require it.

He frowns. She had targeted him?

Or, more precisely, someone had targeted her *at* him.

Who? One of his competitors, trying to distract him?

Ambrose grits his teeth then forces out a laugh. It doesn't matter; he won in the end.

Restless, he flicks absently through the rest of the letters, and only towards the end does he realise that they all begin the same way. "Today, Ambrose stood me up, and there was no moon in the sky", or, "Tonight we walked through the park for hours, talking about our dreams, and the full moon was bright"; always a brief summary of what had happened and a description of the moon, right up until that very last full moon, the night he kissed her.

Strange.

He scans back over the letters, noting how their best dates always coincided with a full moon, and the nights he'd left her hurt the sky had been dark. Curiosity piqued, he reaches for the last letter, unfolds it, and begins to read.

Today, there is no moon. There has been no moon for twenty-one months now and I wonder if you know why.

A shiver finds his spine, and Ambrose rubs the goosebumps from his arms. It's been twenty-one months since he died. Is the moon's disappearance his fault after all?

You're a shadow, but because you were human once, it's enough; life clings to you like oil to water.

I cannot die—but I cannot cling to half-life either. So tonight, there'll be a moon again.

You were human, she says. What is she, then? Absently, he brushes his fingers against his lips, feeling the ghost of hers, and he remembers the light flooding his front step just now.

"There will be a moon again," he murmurs, and his heart contracts. Who is she, that she can predict the moon?

...Then again, so what?

He brushes his nerves aside. She'd no doubt penned the letter right before she came, probably by the light of the very moon she claimed to predict—hardly some feat of prophecy. No. Nothing to worry about, and he is the only immortal, he knows that without a doubt. She's trying to mess with his head, nothing more, and he won't let her.

I don't need you. I never needed you, and certainly not in the way you needed me. But I did love you.

What does she mean, she didn't need him? She shadowed him everywhere, hung on his every word! He was everything to her. He'd *meant* something to her.

The paper crumples in his hand as he presses his fist against the chair, anger clogging his throat. And to say that *he* needed *her*? He'd never needed anyone less. She'd nearly ruined everything.

I'm going home, now. You wouldn't be dissuaded from your goals, and the Fates have decided my job is done. I disagree; I think you'll see the point in time. After all, you have time illimited now, and I think you know that what you sacrificed will always haunt your dreams.

And there it is: she's giving up after all. Good, he thinks, vindictive. Then he reads the paragraph again and is kissed with disappointment. She hadn't loved him after all, despite what she may say. Someone had hired her to draw him away from the quest for immortality. He swallows down the sourness. This is a good thing. It means he didn't hurt her, isn't responsible, because she never truly wanted anything more.

As for the last, well, he has no dreams now. He hasn't dreamed of love or guilt, kindness or anything other than sheer and bloody-minded determination in years.

At least, that's what he tells himself in the early hours of the morning when he wakes, drenched in sweat. Ambrose scowls and pushes the image aside.

You won't hear from me again, the letter continues. *In a few years, you'll probably forget that I ever existed. But I'll be watching you. Because I do love you. You're never alone.*

All that follows is her signature, embellished with a sliver-moon. "Watching me," he mutters, scrambling to his feet. It doesn't occur to him that she might be lying, because that's not the kind of thing she does. Instead, he paces in a circle, wondering where she might be hiding.

But halfway round it hits him: Lena doesn't lie. She's gone, she's never coming back. Tonight, the night he'd finally answered the door for her, she is gone.

He clutches for the curtain and it slides aside. Moonlight floods in and alights on the table where letters and petals are strewn.

Moonlight on petals, the last thing he remembered before he died. Lena in the moonlight, bright-eyed and laughing; Lena in darkness, a figure half glimpsed over his shoulder as he walked away. The moon was always bright when Lena was and always dim when she cried.

A hazy memory struggles into view. It's that night in the park when they confessed secrets to each other and he said things he'd never said before, and never should have then. She'd tried to tell him something, a story about a young woman who was the moon, and he'd laughed, and done like he always had, and brushed her words aside.

Now, he glances between the letters on the table and the full moon in the sky.

From here, he can just make out her signature and its adornment—and the shadows on the moon that look like blossoms.

Blood racing, Ambrose holds his breath all the way to the front door and rests his hand on the knob. "I'm watching you," he whispers. "You're never alone." Palms sweaty, mouth dry, he opens the door. He's cut himself off from everything because he can't bear to walk alone, but what if he doesn't have to? He has so much life left after all.

The street sprawls before him, bathed in silver and black, everything sharp, everything clear. Cherry blossoms wither, but the moonlight is forever. He takes a deep breath, closes his eyes, and steps out into the night.

Perhaps, if it was a more sensational world, the moonlight might ignite his skin and the trees might burst into song. Instead, when he opens his eyes, nothing has changed—only now he knows he doesn't have to face forever alone, imprisoned in an unloved house with an unloved rug, unloved by all the world. Lena may be gone, but she will always be there, just as she always has, and the sky will never be empty again.

WEAVING MAGIC

As you tangle fingers in my untamed hair
lips meet, and
tongues touch, and
you are the sweetness of someone without guile.
Running fingers down my thigh, soft,
like a bird, you weave
magic to make me beautiful, blessing
stretch-marked places,
cellulit places,
not-so-perfectly-tanned places,
places society is ashamed of.
You call me lovely, and I press against
the nakedness of your words,
the brush of your chocolate forelock,
the whisper of rough stubble across my cheek,
the ghost of your hand in mine;
I am beautiful.

24

ANSWER THE QUESTION

I TILTED MY HEAD BACK AGAINST THE PASTEL GREEN WALL OF the day spa, relaxing just enough that I could feel every ache and pain in my body. Man, I was looking forward to this massage.

The door handle on one of the client rooms twisted, and a fraction of a second before the door opened, I stiffened. Heat sang through my body and, furious, I stuffed it away. Not Brandr.

For a brief moment I panicked, wondering if Bianca had mixed things up and booked my massage with him again—but I forced myself to breathe and relax, keeping my eyes closed. Bianca ran her day spa with a golden heart and an iron fist; she wouldn't do that to me.

Still, as Brandr exited the client room and crossed the waiting area, footsteps soft on the rugged floor, I felt more than heard him pause in front of me, every sense in my body standing to rigid attention.

Steady breath in, steady breath out. Steady breath in, steady breath out. I'd managed to successfully ignore him through all of our infrequent encounters since that first massage, and today would be no different.

In front of me, he sniffed. "I clearly need to have a word with Bianca," he muttered, and I couldn't tell if he was including me in his audience or not. "That lounge needs replacing, and some things around here are getting downright old and worn."

I managed to avoid choking on my disbelief until he left the room, though I could still see the back of his head disappearing down the stairs, so doubtless he heard me. Whatever. I didn't even care. Stupid, arrogant, jerk-faced *twat*. Just because he was so pretty that girls fell over themselves to be near him. Well, I wasn't falling for it, even if it *had* been the best bloody massage of my life. I was not some stupid, vapid piece of arm-candy for him to play with. Urgh.

I slammed my head back against the wall just a little too hard, and winced. *Moron. Imbecile! Arrogant peacocky slimeball!*

"Ellie?" Bianca's soothing voice halted my litany and I sighed, forcing away the frustration that encounters with Brandr always left me. "Your turn, honey."

Damn him. I was going to enjoy my massage. He was not going to ruin this perfect moment of relaxation.

Firmly shoving thoughts of stunningly gorgeous manwhores from mind, I followed Bianca into a treatment room.

I slid into my regular seat at Felici's just as Nana and Tanya, my older sister, were handing their menus to the waitress. "I'll have the usual," I said as the waitress raised an eyebrow at me.

She nodded and swept away, leaving behind a cobalt blue bottle that sparkled and dripped with condensation.

"So," I said, pouring water for everyone, "what's new?"

Tanya shrugged. "Nothing much. Working retail during the holiday season still sucks. Though at least

Brandr is on this afternoon, so things won't be deadly boring until he finishes up at six."

The glass I reached for slipped, tipped, and sailed towards the floor. Nana, with characteristic lightning reflexes, caught it before it had barely left the table, setting it upright and relieving me of my water-pouring duties.

"Brandr works at the boutique as well?" I said, aiming for nonchalant.

Nana smirked, and I pointedly ignored her.

Sister nodded. "Oh, yeah. He does mornings in the spa and afternoons downstairs in the storefront."

I made a careful mental note to avoid Schwab in the afternoons. Not that I needed much help with that; Schwab was a designer boutique selling jewellery and cosmetics that were at least four times out of my price range.

I'd known they were affiliated with the day spa, but I hadn't realised they shared staff. I guess it made sense, especially for the cosmetics and beauty product sales.

Whatever. Irrelevant.

I shoved the whole issue aside and turned to Nana. "So, I was thinking of hitting up the department store this afternoon. I need some clothes for work. Do you want to come?"

Not only did Nana have impeccable taste, she also had an almost-bottomless bank account, and she had no qualms about sharing it with her two surviving family members.

She nodded decisively. "Yes," she said. "It will be illuminating."

My eyebrows knitted in puzzlement, but I let it pass. Nana was well known for her bizarre comments and apparently unconnected observations. "Sure," I said. "Thank you."

"Swing by Schwab when you're done," Tanya said, setting her empty glass back on the table. "I'm stuck there till eleven tonight. I'll take my break when you come."

Nana was already agreeing enthusiastically, and I groaned. So much for avoiding the place.

Never mind. We'd go in, find Tanya, and drag her out for a break. The chances of running into Brandr were entirely minimal. Everything would be fine.

"I'll just be a second," I assured Nana as I ducked into the shopping centre bathroom.

We'd spent a good couple of hours clothes-hunting, and all of the resulting outfits were nicer than what I had on now. If we were only stopping past Schwab to collect Tanya, my chances of running into Brandr were minimal (thank heavens), but if we did I wasn't interested in providing more fodder for insults.

Old and tired. Prat.

Locked safely in a stall, I surveyed my options. The navy was too formal; the silver too attention-seeking. I settled on a neutral-toned skirt that showed off my butt and a red silk blouse with fluttery cap sleeves that managed to actually make me look like I had cleavage. The whole outfit was chic yet effortless, the neutral skirt enriching the light brown of my hair and the red blouse the best possible colour for my skin tone.

I pulled it all on, slipped on some gorgeous new heels—it was so shallow of me, but I did love Nana's bank account—fluffed my hair, and headed back out.

Nana whistled. "Don't you look special," she said.

I smiled distractedly, running my fingers along the blouse's neckline.

"It's missing something," I said. "I need something around my neck."

Nana shrugged. "If you say so."

I loaded my bags back into the trolley and marched off determinedly. Three times Nana tried to draw my attention to jewellery stores we passed, but I knew exactly the one I was after.

We rounded the corner: Schwab. Narrowing my eyes, I made a beeline for the main jewellery display in the back of the store.

Nana caught up after a few moments, and eyed the dazzling array of entirely over-the-top necklaces, the lightest of which looking like it had to weigh at least a pound. "These aren't really what you're looking for, dear," she observed candidly.

I shrugged, stifling irritation. "I thought they'd have a bigger range. This one's okay," I added, pointing out a silver filigreed piece with a floral motif.

Voices erupted around the end of the aisle and I froze. *I will not turn around. I will not turn around.* I realised I was checking myself out in the mirror to make sure the outfit was sitting right, and jerked my gaze away. "Or this one." I reached for another necklace to my left, conveniently allowing me to turn my back on the approaching Prince of Twathood.

Nana, of course, turned towards him. "Oh, *I* see. Of course."

Was it permissible to hit grandmothers for being smug? If it had been Tanya, I'd have whacked her for sure.

"I'll just wait out the front, I think," Nana continued, oblivious to my glares. "My feet, you know. And my hips. And my back." She hobbled away to the tables out the front, looking every day of her age—which I'd never seen her do when she wasn't up to mischief.

I was too busy fuming at her retreating back to realise that Brandr had come within range.

"Can I help you?" he said, eyes dancing.

No. I was *not* looking at his stupid pretty eyeballs. I whirled back to the jewellery display. "That one," I said primly. "I'd like to try it on please."

He reached for the necklace that hung just out of my reach, brushing past my shoulder in the process.

I jolted at the energy his touch sent through me and ended up three feet away down the aisle. My stupid reflexes were always a little unpredictable, but they seemed worse when he was around. This had been an utterly ridiculous idea. So what if he thought I looked old and tired? Why did I care what he thought?

"Here."

I turned back to him, expecting to see the silver fili-gree. Instead, he held a ropey, glimmering creation I could have sworn wasn't on the shelves a moment ago. It was a single necklace, but made up of tens or maybe even hundreds of strands; I couldn't quite get a fix on it to figure it out. The threads seemed unnaturally fine and soft, like spider's silk, the beads tiny and delicate as dewdrops.

It glimmered gently in the fluorescent lights of the store, and I stood motionless, transfixed.

"Do you like it?" There was a depth of emotion to Brandr's voice that I'd never heard before, and my heart skipped a beat in response.

"Yes," I breathed, awkwardness and irritation forgotten.

Brandr beamed and my pulse skipped again. Saints, he was beautiful. Too beautiful, like a dangerous snake, but as he moved towards me with the necklace in hand, I was powerless to break the spell.

He reached for me and I turned to face the mirror, my back to him so he could fasten the necklace around my neck. Instead, he laid one end of it across my forehead and directed me to hold it in place while he arranged the rest of the multitude of strands through the back of my hair, half catching it up in a style that seemed at once impossibly complex and incredibly simple.

He fastened the catch on the jewellery just above my left ear and dropped a strand of hair to cover it. I stared at the mirror, lost for words. The necklace—headpiece—whatever it was—had glimmered before, but in my hair it shone. I felt like I was wearing a headdress of moonlight that seemed to pulse gently in time with my breaths.

"Stunning."

I glanced up at Brandr in the mirror, surprised to see his eyes shining wetly. That instant was enough to break the spell though, and I turned. "Let me show Nana," I said. "I mean, let me see what she thinks."

He stepped back, deferential. "Of course."

Out the front of the store I found Tanya engaged in vibrant conversation with Nana, who sat with her back to me. Tanya's eyes widened as she spotted me. She paused mid-sentence. Nana twisted in her chair to see what Tanya had seen—and her hand flew to her mouth.

"Oh," she said as I drew close. "Oh, Elyena. You have it in your hair."

I shrugged, suddenly embarrassed. "Oh, well," I said, tugging on the strands across my forehead. "Brandr thought he'd try something different."

"Brandr did this?" Nana asked. She turned back to her table and busied herself in her copious handbag before I could reply.

Irritated, I snagged the necklace and tugged it down over my face. I shook my hair free from it and twisted it around to hang around my neck. Stupid Brandr and his stupid ideas. What was he playing at, anyway?

"There," I snapped at the table, Tanya already engrossed in a new conversation with Brandr, and Nana still rummaging in her bag. Seriously, would it kill them to focus on me for more than a second? "Now what do we think?"

I twitched the luminous white strands that trailed down my chest, still beautiful, but lacking the glorious allure they'd had in the mirror just before.

Brandr narrowed his eyes critically at me. "The shirt does alluring things to your cleavage, I'll give you that, even if it does emphasise your wide shoulders. I still wish you'd let me trim your hair, your forehead's getting completely lost..." He trailed off under my glare. "No?"

"I *meant* about the *necklace*." My voice was remarkably calm for someone struggling not to commit homicide.

Beside him, Tanya laughed. "I'm sorry. I've been training him for months, and he's still barely housebroken." She turned to him. "Brandr, what's our mantra? Answer the question..."

"Nothing else." He nodded. "Answer the question, nothing else."

They repeated it again together before dissolving into giggles.

I shook my head. "I'll just, uh, go put this back then, shall I?"

"Yes, dear," Nana said. "You can try to do that if you like."

I rolled my eyes at her theatrics and headed for the back of the store. I hunted the display shelf for a place to hang the necklace. Oddly, there didn't seem to be any empty hooks. I ran the necklace through my fingers, glancing down at where it hung limply around my neck. It was pretty—magically so—but it lacked the sparkle, the mysterious something else I'd thought it had when Brandr had first put it on me.

On a whim, I faced the mirror and tugged the necklace back up into my hair, trying to mimic the style Brandr had created. Soft strands fell over my forehead and caught my hair partially up; it wasn't quite how he'd done it, but... I tilted my head at the mirror and my heart skipped a beat.

Hesitantly, I reached up to touch the gossamer strands where they glimmered and glowed like a slipped halo.

Something solid hit me across the backs of my thighs. I flailed wildly for balance and found myself clinging to Brandr's head, as he pranced wildly around the store with me on his shoulders, shouting, "Answer the question, nothing else! Answer the question, nothing else!"

Oh saints, my stomach's showing. I tugged awkwardly at my shirt, caught between fleeting embarrassment and his wildly infectious enthusiasm.

"But what's the question?" I shouted over the din, too disoriented by suddenly being on his shoulders to think of anything better to say.

He laughed. "The necklace! It works!"

"Um, yay?"

Brandr performed some complicated sort of movement that removed me from his shoulders and ended up with me in his arms. "Yay?" he said, eyes oddly serious in contrast to the frivolity of the situation.

"Well," I said, waving my hands as vaguely as I felt, "It works, right? So yay?" I still had no idea what 'working' entailed, but whatever it was, apparently this was Christmas for Brandr.

He hugged me tightly to him and where our skin touched, fire rippled through me. Saints. I'd forgotten what it felt like to have actual proper skin contact with him, not just accidental brushes I did my best to avoid.

It was like drowning, and it was addictive, and it was probably just my imagination that my necklace halo was glowing like it might go nova and Brandr was holding me, touching me, and my hands were wrapping around the back of his neck and through his hair as the air around us burst with perfect, glorious pleasure.

Skin. I needed his skin.

My stomach flipped as something happened to gravity and I had a brief impression of broken plasterboard and a flash of darkness before Brandr lay me down somewhere soft, and all I cared about was the touch of his skin, because it was beautiful, and perfect, and I nearly sobbed as heat soaked through me, lighting up every fibre of my being and chasing out fear and doubt and darkness—except just *there*, in my head, the seat of logic and rationality. *It* remained unmoved, a cold stone trying to catch my attention in the wave of heat.

"Wait," I gasped. I needed a moment to process this.

He ignored me, hands rubbing at my shoulders just like they had that first time in—

I took in the plush-rugged floor, the pastel green walls, the ivory couches around the perimeter of the room. We were in the day spa. I struggled semi-upright. "Wait! How on earth did we..."

He paused, and I found the gaping hole in the floor. Vague memories of a surge of power, of Brandr springing upwards ten metres or more to the roof—*through* the roof—through the *floor*... I stared at him, wide-eyed, the magma flow of heat suddenly halted. "What are you?"

"Happy," he mumbled against my shoulder.

I whacked him gently on the back of the neck. "Answer the question," I said.

"Nothing else," he murmured, nuzzling my neck. My skin fizzed where his lips touched, and I had to concentrate to rap him on the back of the head.

"Yes," I said. "Nothing else."

He sat back, eyes clouded with lust slowly clearing. "I am what you are, Love: a child of the gods. Well, I am closer than you: my mother was a goddess. Your grandmother is the actual godling in your family."

My heart stalled. Child of the gods? Me? *Nana*?

Actually, I had to admit that made a hell of a lot of sense. Nana's bizarre observations, her uncanny sense of timing, her ridiculous physical abilities...

I blinked, unsure what was more unsettling: that my grandmother was a godling, or that it was dead easy to believe it.

"Hold on, wait," I said, wriggling further out from underneath Brandr. "If you're a godling, then..." I hesitated, not sure how to phrase my question, and not sure I wanted to know the answer.

A godling. No wonder girls of all ages threw themselves at him. How many women had he loved in his lifetime? Ten? Twenty? A hundred?

Cold logic was almost as good as a cold shower.

"No," I said. "No."

"No what?"

"No as in I-am-*not*-going-to-be-the-latest-in-a-long-line-of-floozies-no." I shook my head. "Not interested. I don't care what you are, I'm not available."

His eyes widened, body and face alike drooping in disappointment. "But Love, you feel it, I know you do."

"Feel what?" I snapped, arms wrapped tightly around my torso. I felt nothing that he didn't manipulate me to feel with his stupid godly powers.

"This," he whispered, and reached out.

His fingertip connected softly with the corner of my jaw, and I swallowed against the melting heat that tried to consume me.

His finger trailed down my neck, tracing a blissful line across the hollow of my clavicle, lighting fire oh-so-carefully down my sternum.

He pulled away and I remembered how to breathe.

"See?" he said, still whispering. "How can you deny it?"

I shook my head, tears burning my eyes. *I don't want this, I don't want this,* I reminded myself frantically. "It isn't real."

My nails dug into my palms as I stared into his sea-green eyes, so full of sadness they seemed a mirror of my own. "Tell me..." I drew in a shaky breath. "Answer the question."

He nodded, gaze searching my face like an enigma.

"How many other girls?"

Brandr frowned, and sadness turned to confusion.

I rolled my eyes, flicking away tears with a quick finger. "Don't give me that. How many other girls have you played this game with, made... feel like this?"

I wasn't holding my breath for his answer. I wasn't.

His confusion deepened. "But Love, I couldn't."

It was my turn to be confused. "What do you mean?"

He shook his head. "I couldn't *make* someone feel like this. When I touch you, I feel what you feel. I felt it that first time, do you remember? The massage?"

Saints, how I had tried to forget. His touches had been perfectly innocent, utterly professional, but the fire they'd awoken in me had left me reeling in terror; I'd never felt anything so strong in my life.

A tiny smile played at the corners of his mouth. "That's when I knew."

My heart pounded in my head, my chest... "Knew what?"

He was leaning closer, lips a mere breath away, and I didn't want to be a conquest, but now that I thought about it—really and truly thought about it, without the filter of frustration and jealousy—could it be? Was I really the only girl actually losing her head over this man, the only one struggling not to throw herself at his feet?

"I knew," he whispered against my ear, and I almost couldn't hear him through the ecstasy echoing through my body, "that you were the one."

"I don't believe in soulmates," I whispered back, eyes closed, every sense in my body standing to attention as his cheek tickled against mine.

"You don't have to." His lips traced my jaw and I shivered. "Your heart recognises me, Love, whether you believe in it or not."

"Love," I whispered, fingers tightening in his hair. "Is that what this is?"

"Not yet," he said. "But it could be. If you wanted it to be."

I luxuriated in the thought for just a moment, before another one hit me. I bolted upright, narrowly avoiding a collision with his nose. "Wait just one second here, buddy. Old? You think I look tired and old?" His words from that morning rang in my ear. "Not to mention, oh, I don't know, my too-broad shoulders and my totally-lost forehead!" I glared at him, wishing that godling powers included the ability to set someone literally on fire.

Brandr laughed, a soft, throaty chuckle that sounded far too appealing. "I knew you'd take it like that, and I confess, I half hoped I'd provoke you into responding. But if you recall, I said that *some* things around here were getting downright old and worn. I mean, Love, your constant indifference. Not *you*."

He tracked a finger over my hairline, leaving tingling fireworks in its wake.

"That's nice," I said, pushing his hand away, "But what about my shoulders? And my forehead?"

He frowned, confusion plain again. "What about them?"

"You..." I squirmed, uncertain how to voice my fears aloud without sounding insecure and needy. "They're not 'too broad', and, well, you know...?"

"Look at me, Love," he said. "Am I perfect?"

YES, my heart screamed. YES YOU ARE BLOODY PERFECT. But I shoved the scrambling emotions away and forced myself to look.

Cold logic; cold shower; I could do this. And true, now he mentioned it, his nose leaned a bit to one side, and one eye was slightly larger than the other, and if I was going to be utterly picky then his forehead was probably a fraction too large, and... "Oh."

Brandr softened into a smile. "Answer the question, Love."

"Yes," I said. "And no. I see what you mean. You mean that—"

He pressed a finger against my lips. "Answer the question, Love, but nothing else." His eyes sparkled.

I smiled.

He leaned down and kissed me, and this time, I kissed him back.

BUT FOR SNOW

THE MARKET IS TOO BRIGHT—TOO MANY PEOPLE SHOUTING, laughing, singing—and Tundra cringes, shrugging her shoulders up around her ears. The place is raucous; it makes her head hurt. The smell of cinnamon and hot oil smothers her nose from the food vendors' stalls, and the sunshine is fierce, making the damp ground humid and suffocating everyone with a hot, sapping afternoon.

Tundra wanders away a few steps, carefully eyeing her mother as she busies herself at a stall full of twisted metal jewellery. Tundra creeps a few steps more, the soft grass tussocks compressing under her feet as though they too are trying to be quiet in the hubub of the crowd.

She reaches the corner unnoticed, peeks back to see only her mother's fuchsia silk headscarf through the crush and bustle.

Tundra runs. If she runs fast enough, the people blur and even though it's noisy still, it's nearly as good as being alone. The rumble of the crowd is like the wind that whips her long hair and tickles her ears, and she laughs from deep in her belly because if she can just run fast enough, it's almost like flying.

Tundra pauses in the liminal space of a side-alley where the evening sun doesn't reach. She sobers; others give the alley a wide berth. Dark shadows clutch cages against the walls and the breeze that gusts from the bowels of the alley is cold and full of night, and the smell of old, dry things. Tundra peers warily, curiosity piqued by the multitude of eyes that reflect the dim light. She has always liked animals.

Tundra glances over her shoulder as goosebumps prickle her skin. Her heart hammers, not in fear of the inhuman night, but that someone might see her, might tell her she shouldn't be here. People are always telling her she shouldn't be in the places she wants to go.

The wind stirs her hair into wisps, ghost fingers teasing in the dark. Tundra tucks her hair firmly behind her ears and enters the alley, lungs filling with the dry-fur smell as she breathes deeply.

Iron-barred cages skulk in corners, and smaller wicker cages dance on ropes crisscrossing overhead, knocking hollowly in the breeze.

"Hello, pretty thing," Tundra says softly as she approaches the nearest cage, stretching out her fingers for its occupant to sniff.

The creature backs away and shivers, fur softly silver in the dim light, eyes wide and yellow.

Tundra holds the bars of the cage and wants to cry. Animal thoughts are not like human thoughts—they lack the words—but she can feel that the creature does not like its cage; it remembers skies, and treetops, and rain.

Something shrieks. Tundra whips around, adrenalin pulsing through her.

Perched on a cage above her head is a large, velvety black bird with snowy white chest feathers. Tundra moves closer, standing on tiptoes to see. The bird's beak is huge and it's so brightly coloured that Tundra wonders if someone has painted it. Then she sees the chain binding the bird's leg and her chest knots up again.

"I'm sorry," she whispers to the bird, bundling up her pity and sending it in a way the bird will understand. "My mother tries to keep me caged up too."

It isn't fair.

Something shifts in the crate below the bird and Tundra crouches. The crate is deep in shadow, and her eyes tell her it's empty, but she knows her eyes are wrong. She can feel the thoughts of the creature inside and watches carefully, waiting for the moment when it will reveal itself. "It's all right," she croons. "I won't hurt you."

There. A shadow darker than the rest, a hint of fur, a paw.

Tundra smiles. "See? That wasn't so hard." She kneels on the smooth-worn cobbles, waiting for the creature to throw off its shadow cloak entirely.

White fur catches the faint light. It is a wolf, half-grown, curled tightly nose to tail.

He opens his eyes, piercing Tundra with his ice-blue gaze.

She gasps, because deep within that gaze lies recognition.

He knows who she is.

She knows who *he* is.

And yet, of course, she doesn't.

He's only a wolf, with strange blue eyes and a cloak woven of darkness. But he *feels*... he feels like her dreams, the strange ones of ice and snow she's had as long as she can recall, the ones with a sense of something missing so strong it takes her breath away just remembering it.

The wolf cub looks like he would enjoy those dreams, Tundra thinks.

It's a simple enough matter to pick the cold iron lock with some splinters of wood and piece of wire off the ground, and although her heart hammers and her palms grow sweaty, no one approaches, no one asks her business.

After a minute or two, the door creaks open. The gangly cub stretches, undulating his back and ending with a shake of his tail. He yawns, twitches his black-tipped ears and stares up at her.

Her breath catches in her throat at the gaze of an apex predator—but he will not harm her, she thinks. He...

She swallows. He feels like the thing that has been missing from her dreams.

His tail wafts and his mouth opens in a grin.

Does he feel it too, the sense that this is a meeting long foretold? Only one way to know. Tundra walks away, glancing back at the cub.

He follows. Tundra breaks into a trot, then a run as she leaves the alley behind for the bright sunlight and warm smells of the streets. The cub keeps pace and together they run right to the edge of town, out to the plains of warm, sweet-smelling grasses—and some-how, this is how it's always been. But for want of snow, this could be her dreams come true.

The moon, full to bursting as it dips toward the horizon, reminds Tundra that her mother will be looking for her. She glances down at the wolf, unable to bear the thought of going home tonight without him. She's only just found him, the missing piece of her dreams.

And besides, she hates the house. It's not a special loathing, just discomfort born of a preference for solitude, for cold, for wide-open spaces.

The wolf stares up at Tundra and her breath catches in her throat. She reaches out and touches him for the first time. His fur, white but for his silvery-grey back and black-tipped ears, is cold. Tundra's heart leaps and she grins, half mad with the thought of her own cold wolf. His fur burns her fingertips like ice and she luxuriates, sinking her fingers right down to his skin.

The cub snaps playfully at the air and Tundra laughs, pouncing on him. They wrestle, growing careless, and Tundra suddenly feels his teeth. She freezes, stunned.

The cub whines and backs away, ears and tail low.

Tundra shakes her head. "It's okay," she murmurs, reaching out to him with her good hand—because the one he bit is not a good hand any longer: it's marked with a perfect row of round tooth-punctures, each one filled with ice. She rubs at them, but the ice will not melt. They look like a string of diamonds over the side of her hand.

The cub whines again and Tundra tussles his ears fiercely. "I like it," she insists, and he nuzzles his face against her as though he would lick her if he could.

Worn out, Tundra lies back in the grass and stares at stars that sparkle bright and brittle, promising winter. The cub curls up at her side and falls asleep, and although her mother will be furious, Tundra cannot bear to wake him.

Wrapped in cold and frost and the smell of fur, she falls asleep, and together they dream of ice and snow, and games played in the chilly breeze of death.

In the morning, the wolf cub is gone. The same sense of loss from her dreams floods over Tundra, and she lies still, her heart broken.

Mother. She will be livid. Tundra sighs and hauls herself to her feet—and the cub comes bounding to her side. He prances beside her, batting at butterflies, fur glistening in the early morning light.

Tundra grins, relieved. Mother won't let him stay with her at the house, but that doesn't matter. Tundra is an expert at hiding things from her family—and with six older siblings, that's no mean feat. But she takes the wolf to a pen of branches hidden in the forest behind the house in a thicket of boxalder, and feels confident that no one will come across him there.

Mother scolds her something fierce when Tundra creeps in the back door. Tundra cowers and makes innocent eyes at her, and Mother sighs in frustration. "Here," she says, handing Tundra a dishcloth. "You're on pots."

Tundra nods meekly and counts down the minutes as she spends her morning up to her elbows in the wreckage of her mother's latest canning spree.

It's lunchtime before she can escape back to her wolf, and as she nears the pen he howls. Tundra curls her fists, telling herself that her nails pressing into her palm are payment for the pain she hears in her wolf's cry.

Tundra's heart leaps when she sees the pen: the branches are turned to ice, and in one corner the wolf has nearly broken through.

She hesitates. Perhaps the wolf is not really hers, but wild. Perhaps she dreamed their bond. But one look in his eyes reassures her, and she sets about replacing ice with wood, crooning and soothing him as she works. He rubs against her and grins, tongue lolling to the side, and Tundra's shoulders lift. *See?* she tells her herself. *He is happy here.*

Once the pen is repaired, she pets him for a while, rubbing his ears between her fingers and scratching at the base of his tail. "I'll always come back," she tells him. "I promise. You mustn't fret while I'm gone. We're bonded now, and I must take care of you." She nods decisively. She will take care of him. She will.

Tundra trudges back to the house, where more chores await.

Snow-thoughts haunt the rest of her day.

At dusk she sneaks out again, and once more she must replace the walls of the pen.

The wolf is listless, but Tundra refuses to see that his eyes are duller, his gaze less piercing. She tussles his ears. "I can't sleep with you tonight, Snow Wolf. Mother will have my hide if I'm not in bed all night, and I know her: she'll come to check. But I'll be back as soon as I can in the morning. I promise."

The wolf whines as she hurries away, but she shakes her head and pretends it's nothing more than the wind whistling through the trees.

That night, for the first time since she can remember, Tundra does not dream of snow. She wakes with sandy eyes and a headache, feeling as she did the time her brother Thiel tricked her into drinking a large mug of Father's best ale. She drags herself out of bed and down to see the wolf, who stays curled in a corner of his pen and won't come near her, won't even stand.

Tundra's nails bite into her palms again. "I hate it just as much as you do," she mutters. "I'd much rather we could both roam free. But they'd kill you if they saw you. You're a wolf."

And Mother has told her on pain of bedroom imprisonment that she is not to wander off today, and because Tundra hates her room so much, she won't. "I'm sorry," she says to the wolf.

As she leaves, he howls.

Tundra spends the morning cramped in the confines of the laundry, chained to the washtub, scrubbing out clothes on the board.

By the time Mother calls her for lunch, her hands are wrinkled and pale as though they haven't seen the sun in days, and she feels about the same. The walls of the house close in on her and she feels irritable, like someone is watching her over her shoulder. But she slides her lunchmeat into her lap anyway, and bundles it up for the wolf.

Tundra dangles the meat over the edge of the pen, trying to entice the wolf. "Here, wolfie," she singsongs. "Nice wolfie." He ignores her.

Tundra throws the meat into the dirt and stomps away. "Stupid dog," she mutters.

She doesn't eat dinner that night, doesn't dream of snow.

"Chores today?" Tundra says over-brightly as she joins her mother in the kitchen.

Mother blinks in surprise. "If you like." She sets Tundra enough work to occupy her until the evening shadows begin to lengthen and the trees reach out to tangle their branches in the sun.

As Mother begins preparations for dinner, Thiel strides through the yard.

The movement catches Tundra's eye, and she glances up, only for the bottom to drop out of her world.

It's like she is falling, or drowning, or perhaps the walls are closing in and she is suffocating, because slung over her brother's left shoulder, perfect counter-point to the rifle over his right, hangs a wolf, gangly and long-limbed like a half-grown cub.

It is only as Thiel has nearly disappeared that Tundra sees the wolf's eyes, glassy and staring, are yellow.

She drags in a shaky breath, removes her apron, and dashes through the yard. Fear and hope war in her chest, making it hard, so hard, to breathe.

At last she pushes into the thicket and the scene is exactly as she hoped—exactly as she feared: the wolf is curled in the same corner as always, his coat matted, his eyes dull.

The meat from yesterday still lies in the dust and ants busy themselves with devouring it. Tundra jumps the fence and kicks at the meat. "It's not your food!" she screams at the ants. "It's not for you!"

And she isn't quite sure if the last is directed at the ants, or the wolf—or herself. But the dreams. The dreams were real—weren't they?

The wolf still hasn't moved, and although she tries not to, Tundra thinks she can see his ribs. She throws the meat at him and storms away.

"Stupid wolf. Eat."

Tundra stomps into the house, ignoring as her father calls her to dinner. She is vaguely aware of her mother murmuring, but she doesn't really hear, doesn't really care.

In her room, she flings herself on the bed face down and drags a blanket over her head. Why won't the wolf eat? She *knows* it's hard being confined, but *she* does it, *she* tolerates it, because one day, she'll be old enough and she won't have to.

The wolf is just a baby still. They're meant to be together. How can they be together if he won't stay penned?

He can't die. He can't.

Tundra drifts off into an uneasy sleep, waking just as twilight fades. She stares at the darkening roof and sighs. She misses her dreams of snow.

Tundra hesitates at the doorjamb, staring out into the night. Her heart pounds and fear is eating her belly alive. *I don't want to,* she thinks. *I don't want to!* Eyes closed, she tries to feel the snow dream. Nothing but emptiness. She misses the dream so much it hurts, and that hurt is just a little bigger than the fear.

She grits her teeth. She must. Tundra pulls off the outer layers of her dress until she's in her shift and nothing more. This part wasn't planned, but as the breeze caresses her, raising goosebumps, she smiles grimly at the cold. Her body may protest, but the cold makes her alive; the cold is of the dream.

When she reaches the pen, Tundra doesn't look at the wolf. She doesn't want to see what might be reflected in his eyes—guilt, pity, or worse, nothing at all. Instead, she grabs the closest branch and tugs it away with an almighty crack. The sound is like her heartstrings snapping, and she claws at the fence in a fury. How dare they be contained. How dare they not roam free, she and her wolf. One day the world will pay for this imprisonment. One day, there will be no fences that can stop them.

Before long, the gap is wide enough for the wolf to fit through. Tundra turns back to the house, still refusing to look, and walks away. If he's still there in the morning, well, then she'll do whatever might need to be done. But if he is anything like her, freedom hard won will restore his soul better than anymore assistance she could offer him.

A crackle of leaves as she nears the end of the thicket draws her involuntary glance. It's the wolf, stepping gingerly out of the pen. His matted fur sheds before Tundra's eyes and new hair glistens in its place. The wolf whines once then leaps into the air, dancing. Tundra jumps too, breathing more easily than she has in days, and for a fleeting instant it could be her dream, but for the lack of snow. Then the wolf lands, whuffs, and lopes away. Tundra wipes the too-warm tears from her cheeks and closes her eyes, searching for the dream.

The wolf howls, and she sees it: she and her wolf, dancing with death in the soft-falling snow.

Tundra nods and, scrubbing at her cheeks, squares her shoulders. As she heads for the house, her wolf howls one last time, already far away, his voice as sharp and brittle as ice.

Tundra's vision is filled with a flurry of snowflakes that feather away all worries, all walls, all fences.

She smiles, chest light. One day, she and her wolf will dance again—and it will snow.

PRIESTS OF THE SANDRINGHAM LINE

They enter under vow of silence,
dressed in black
business suits and skirts and
I am out of place,
in my jeans
and polar-fleece hoodie
and green canvas bag.
Yet together, we join in silent prayer,
heads bowed to the god
of finance, who drives us
by necessity
from our sleep at this early hour.
They sway and dance
and the woman's sequin-beaded
handbag with the stylised strawberry
glitters like an offering, a sacrifice
bought to please an ever-hungry deity.
The carriage stops;
priests scatter to their houses
of worship, and are replaced,
and the carriage clacks
onwards, carrying priests
of the Sandringham line.

ALONE

He LINGERS OVER HIS APPROACH TO THE FRONT DOOR, breathing deeply, filling his dry, creaky lungs with the scent of home. Stone and damp, old tomatoes and dust. His life encapsulated by a perfect smell.

And he'll never smell it again. The soulbond is drawing to an end, he can feel it, feel the weight lifting. Two days, he estimates. Two days and the bond will be gone. He'll be alone for the first time in years.

He casts his gaze over the two storeys of the little house, crammed in at the end of a high-walled alleyway—and yet the only place he's ever been able to breathe. The gang—his family, the ones he chose and raised—are like that. They kept him going when there was nothing else to live for.

He winces. What is he thinking? They need him, his protection—and he needs them. He pauses stiffly on the front step, rubbing the age from his knuckles and the pain from his face.

He opens the door and Tara storms out into the hall. She attacks the stairs without even a glance in his direction. His mouth bunches tightly as he suppresses a laugh. Oh, yes. This is home.

He steps inside and closes the door behind him, smoothing a hand over wood more worn than he is. He takes another deep breath, basking in the warm smells of oak and brass polish.

A sigh, from the living room. Is that her? Fortuitous, if so. The more of them he can avoid today the better. Dying is hard enough without having to say goodbye.

Especially when one must die alone.

He creeps across the hallway, floorboards gently protesting, and pauses for a moment in the doorway to drink in the scene. The bay window to his left lets in the little light available in this bottom storey of a back alley, softly illuminating the furniture older than he is—and probably in better condition. His lips twitch in a half smile.

And there, curled in the single armchair by the fireplace, bathed in flickering firelight, sits Jessana. He smiles at the contradiction of the literary novel in her hand and the assassin's knife lying on the table next to her, loving it even as he hates himself for nurturing the killer in her. But it had been necessary, a choice of her life, the life of his almost-daughter, against the lives of faceless, impersonal others. He'd kept her alive by teaching her his skills.

He tenses, thinking of what he is about to do; it feels precariously like abandoning her. Pain stabs at his ribcage. He sucks in air that tastes like age and smooths the mask over his face. They will never know about the pain—but the goodbye he can't delay much longer. So he straightens from the wall, squares his shoulders, and enters the room.

Jess glances up and smiles. "Hello!" She unfurls her legs to get to her feet, but he waves her back down.

"No need for that." He lowers himself into a nearby chair and nods at her clenched fist. "What have you got there?"

Jess sighs and rolls her eyes, putting down her book and offering her other hand. "Tara found it."

"Unusual." The glossy black ring seems the antithesis of Jess, shrouded in darkness as she is haloed in light. For a moment he feels as though it tugs at his soulbond; but the moment passes, and it is just a ring, if an unusually deep black one.

"Very," Jess responds. "And I don't even want to know where she got it from, especially if it's where I think she did."

"And where might that be?"

"A dead body."

"Oh, Jess," he says, laughing. "You've got your hands full with that one." He grins; Jess grins back.

"Is there any hope?" she asks in mock despair.

He sobers. "Funny you should say that," he murmurs. "I was just thinking the other day that she reminded me of someone." He shoots Jess a significant look.

She responds with a wry smile. "Okay," she says. "I give in. I'll persevere with the little monster."

He chuckles. "Good girl."

The silence stretches.

Jess glances at her novel, then back at him. "Did you want something?"

It's time. It has to be done. His mind races for things to say, anything other than what needs to be said.

Nothing comes, so he inhales and begins. "Yes, Jessana, I do want something."

Her body language changes, becoming more alert. "Is everything all right?"

He smiles. "Everything is fine. In... in a manner of speaking. You see, it appears that I have..." He swallows, almost choking on the lie. "I have a son."

Jess jerks in surprise.

"Yes," he continues, finding his rhythm. "I was somewhat shocked myself to discover it. But the main point is, he is quite unwell, and his mother is unable to support them with all his medical expenses." A slight pause before the climax of the lie. "I loved his mother very much. I... I have found a job." He stares at the floor, sick to the stomach. "I'm going to live with them, and support them."

He risks a glance at Jess, whose shock is written on her face. Shock, but not disbelief. That's a good sign.

He presses on, the hardest part behind him. "The house will need a new leader, Jessana. I want that leader to be you."

"Me?" she says, incredulous. "Why me? There are others much better qualified. River is the eldest, choose him! Or Patty, she knows how to get everyone moving. Or Alek, or..." She flounders. "Why me?"

He smiles gently. "It has always been you, Jessana. From the moment you arrived. Don't you notice how they follow you?"

The whole world worships the ground you walk on, he doesn't add.

Jess squirms. "I suppose so..."

He takes her hand. "They will support you. Never alone, remember? Do it for me?" He blinks back the tears that threaten to clog his eyes. Their motto, everything they live by—but he has to throw it away. He can't cling to false hope, can't risk having the bond transfer to someone he loves when he passes on.

Jess nods, exhaling. "Okay," she says. "For you."

"Then good." He claps his hands once together and smiles. "That's settled." He makes to rise.

"When do you leave?" Jess says softly, and he feels her eyes probing his facade for the truth, pinning him back in his chair.

He shakes off her gaze, stands and closes his eyes; turns away from love and comfort and joy.

"It's today, isn't it?" she says.

He nods.

"Oh."

And she is there, beside him, wrapping her arms around him, and the tears that he'd promised he wouldn't shed are coursing down his cheeks, making rivulets to rival his wrinkles.

Slowly, her soothing works its way into the crevices of his soul and the tears subside like dust settling to the ground. Jess pats him on the shoulder. "You should go, then," she says. "Wouldn't want to be late, now, would we?"

He smiles, a false, brittle thing that he erases before it cracks his fragile exterior. He flees to the front door and jerks it open, determined not to look back. He steps out, pulls the door—but Jess catches it and props it open, standing to watch him leave.

He walks away down the alley. Midway, Jess calls. "Wait!"

He steels himself, knowing he can't deny her the chance for goodbye. He tenses as he meets her gaze, so piercing he thinks it might kill him there and then.

"Wait," she says again.

"Yes, Jessana?"

"How much longer do you have to live?"

And there it is, the very thing he's been trying to avoid, the reason he'd concocted the story of the job and the family in the first place. And despite it all, in spite of all his acting and plotting and planning—she knows. She still knows.

He works his tongue to moisten his suddenly dry mouth. "Not... Not much longer," he says in a voice that rasps like dead leaves.

"How long?"

Those eyes. Stars of Fate, those eyes... He presses his own closed and forces the words out. "Two days."

The silence and curiosity opens his eyes. Their gazes lock, and she nods. "Two days. Stay nearby. I'll find you."

"You can't!" he says, hands clenching. "I won't have the bond jump to you!"

Jess smiles sadly. "It can't. I'm already bound."

He reels like she's slammed the door in his face. Jess, his precious, perfect Jess, is soulbound too. No wonder she'd seen through his lies.

He nods. "Nearby." She deserves that much. He turns to leave.

"Wait."

Something thuds into the ground behind his feet, and he glances down. Her knife. His gaze flicks to Jess.

"For the pain," she says.

He nods and picks up the knife. "For the pain." Tucking it into his belt, he walks out of the alleyway for the last time.

Behind him, words echo down the street that smells like home. "Never alone, Guiro. Never alone."

INTERCHANGE

"THAT'S RIDICULOUS, JAMES!" ELLA said into her mobile, grateful there was no one else at the bus stop to hear her. The traffic whooshed past on the four-lane road, kicked up the smell of hot asphalt and petrol fumes. "I think I'm capable of running my own life, thanks." She glanced up at the approaching bus juddering its way toward her—an old one, all orange and sky blue.

"Look," she said. "I've got to go. I've *no* doubt we'll discuss this later. Bye."

She hung up on James, thinking as she did how irritating he was becoming. This was the third time he'd expressed disapproval over her plans to go down the coast the weekend before exams. As if the break wouldn't settle her nerves.

She shook her head in disgust.

The bus doors hissed open as it stopped, sending the smell of oil and hot hydraulics into the back of Ella's throat as she stepped up inside.

"Student, please," she said curtly. Ignoring the driver's brief glance at her cleavage, she scanned the bus for an empty seat. The bus stank of old sweat and musty upholstery, nearly full with students and old folk on the way home from bingo. And of course, the occasional middle-aged drifter, taking up space. And leering, like they had the chance to do anything more than look. Ella snorted in disgust.

She spied a seat, halfway down on the left side, and swept down the aisle, flinging herself onto the worn blue seat and wishing, yet again, that she could afford a car.

Scooting over against the window, her thoughts returned to James.

How dare he, she thought. *It's my life, it's my money, I can go away if and when I please, thank you very much.*

Perhaps it was time for a change. She'd been seeing James for what, like two months now? She nodded to herself. That guy in her English class was pretty cute. *Ben. I think he's Ben.*

The bus arrived at the interchange, interrupting her musings. Half of the passengers disembarked and a new horde of students climbed on to take their place.

The last passenger caused Ella to wrinkle her nose —yet another middle-aged man. Briefly, she wondered why there were so many of them on the buses.

Why do these losers not have cars?

The latest specimen headed her way and realisation hit her: the only free seat left was next to her.

She set her handbag firmly on the seat, and shook her head. He didn't seem to see her.

He slid in without a word of apology, a skinny shell of a man taking up far less than half the seat.

The handbag sat like an immutable barrier between them. Ella stared resolutely out the window, hoping that her new companion didn't have too far to travel. She was a good half hour away from her stop, but if he was still there when she had to get off... Well, the last thing she needed was another middle-aged man staring at her butt.

She shuddered slightly at the thought, and examined him out of the corner of her eye. He didn't really look like the butt-staring type, but sometimes they didn't. He was on a bus, after all.

She was about to resume her internal rant at James when—horror of all horrors—the man began to cry. Just softly, and Ella looked around in a covert panic to see if anyone else had noticed.

No one else has noticed, he probably doesn't expect me *to notice, it's all okay, just ignore him.* She stared out the window.

Ella decided that he mustn't have any tissues, as she couldn't think of any other reason why he would sniff so horribly. For a moment, she almost felt sorry for him. Then she remembered that she still didn't know how far he was travelling, and the sympathy faded.

Soon enough, though, the man leaned forward to push the 'stop' button. The purple light up the front of the bus came on. Ella sagged in relief. No butt-staring after all.

She lurched forward as the bus jolted to a stop. The doors opened, and the purple light winked out. The man wiped his face and slid into the aisle.

The doors closed and the bus pulled back into the traffic before Ella glanced down, and noticed the black leather wallet on the seat.

Ella sat on her bed in her plain white t-shirt and pastel tartan pyjama shorts, stroking her tabby rescue cat and staring at the wallet. *To open, or not to open, that is the question*, she thought, proud of herself for actually remembering something from high school.

The scent of the oils in her Versace warmer filled the room, bright and fresh and sunshiney, somewhat at odds with her mood.

"Well, I can't keep it forever, can I, Smudge?" She scratched the tabbycat behind the ear and reached for the wallet.

It was soft, worn, and smelled pleasantly of treated leather.

The driver's licence revealed that the crying man was a Mr Edward Hampton, of Lilac Street, Watson.

Driver's licence? Ella wondered. *He has a licence?* "Why the heck was he on the bus then, Smudgie?" She shook her head, and continued shuffling.

Twenty dollars cash, healthcare card, bank card, credit card, photos of a woman with mid-length wavy brown hair—quite lovely—and a baby—round and pudgy, with brown fuzz instead of hair. Library card, Subway discount card—bus ticket.

Bus ticket.

"Smudge," Ella addressed the cat, holding him up to look into his eyes. "I'm puzzled. Why would anyone in their right mind catch a bus when they could drive? For that matter," she said, putting the cat down and gathering the cards back into the wallet, "why would someone catch a bus if they were going to cry?"

She lay back, staring at the poster on the far wall. "Well," she said, "looks like I'm off to Watson tomorrow. Down you go." She lifted the cat onto the floor, switched off her lamp and snuggled under the covers.

Ella knocked on the plain front door of the tiny house, crammed in elbow-to-elbow amid identical, grey-rendered neighbours, running through what she was going to say in her head. She still wasn't convinced this was the right thing to do—should have just handed it in to the bus company's lost property or something—but she was filled with a curiosity she couldn't quite explain.

The woman from the photo answered the door, with the baby on her hip. "Hello?"

"Hi," said Ella brightly, trying to hide her nerves. "My name's Ella. Mr Hampton left his wallet on the bus yesterday." She held it out as proof.

The woman exhaled with relief. "Why thank you, Ella, that was thoughtful of you to return it."

Ella blushed. She fidgeted, wanting to ask, wanting to know—*Why he was crying? On a bus, of all places?*—but uncertain how to begin.

"Is there anything else?" the woman asked, friendly and welcoming.

"Um, well…" Ella faltered. "It's just that on the bus…" She sighed and met the woman's gaze. "Is he okay?"

The woman's smile disappeared. "He's dying."

Ella flung herself onto her king single bed and stared up at the ceiling.

Dying. The Man was Dying.

She thought in capitals, unable to better express the weight that she perceived in the situation. Megan stuck her head into the room— "Dinner's ready!"—but Ella just nodded absently.

Megan gave her an odd look, then retreated to ga-lumph down the stairs, two at a time.

Dying.

Ella closed her eyes.

'What of?' she had blurted in shock. 'If you don't mind me asking, of course,' she added in a clumsy attempt to soften her bluntness.

'Cancer,' the woman had replied. 'Bowel cancer. We have known for a while, but we thought he was impro-ving.' She looked away. 'He saw the doctors yesterday. He has about eight months left.'

"Dinner!" Dad yelled out from downstairs.

Sighing, Ella rolled over. As she did she brushed against the photo frame on her bedside table. James. She lifted the picture up and stared at it.

The bus chugged along, its uneven gait shaking Ella as she sat, lost in thoughts about the coming day's classes. As it pulled in to a stop, Ella glanced up with mild curiosity to see who would get on. Just one pas-senger at this stop, a middle-aged man.

Moron, Ella thought—and then caught herself. Si-lently, she amended it: M*aybe the car's broken, like the Hampton's*, she thought, hoping as she did that the Hamptons would be able to have theirs fixed soon.

She sighed as this new man passed her, smelling faintly of cheap men's deodorant as he did. *Maybe he's dying.*

The thrum of the engine droned into her head, numbing her from the world. She could see things through the windows, watch people as they went about their lives, but the noise was like a barrier between her and the outside world. Nothing reached her, nothing connected with her. Staring blankly she remembered again:

The woman—Viola—had invited her inside.

'How do you cope?' Ella had asked. 'How do you live, like, going through each day, knowing what the outcome's going to be, but, like, you have to do the boring, daily stuff anyhow?'

Viola stared into space for a moment. She came back with a small shake of her head. 'I don't know Ella. I really don't. I mean, I feel like I haven't even absorbed it yet, not really. And what choice do I have? Whatever happens, I still have little Josh here,' she bounced the baby on her lap, 'and I have a responsibility to him not to curl up and hide.' She sighed. 'I just don't know.'

The bus jerked to a halt and, grabbing her bag, Ella joined the queue of students waiting to exit. Ahead of her a guy with scraggly blonde hair hanging over his eyes jumped down the steps and turned, offering his hand to the girl behind him. The girl smiled shyly, and took his hand.

Nice to see chivalry isn't dead, Ella thought. And sighed. *Dead.*

She sat in her class, thinking. She hadn't heard a word the lecturer had said, but her pen hadn't stopped moving as she spilled out a torrent of words, attempting to make sense of what had happened in the last twenty-four hours.

Mr Hampton is dying. Dying. Why do I feel so shocked at that? People die, things die all the time… but dying… I'm dying. Sally's dying. Mum's dying, Dad's dying, even Megan is dying. Living is dying.

James is dying.

James is dying. Why do I care?

He loves me.

He's overprotective and irritating. He's smothering me, telling me what to do all the time.

He loves me, and wants to make me happy. And he smells like peaches.

He wants to be with me.

Do I want to be with him?

He's a nice guy. Clever. Protective.

He's dying.

…

One chance at love.

One first chance, anyway.

Am I wasting his?

Ella sighed deeply, and recalled again Viola's words —*I have a responsibility not to curl up and hide.*

She wrote a word in capitals on her page:

HIDING.

And underlined it.

HIDING.

Carefully, she amended it once more:

Stop HIDING.

The lecture finished, and en masse the students packed up and left, the scent of garlic bread and hot chips wafting in from the food court outside as the double doors swung in and out, in and out.

Ella sighed, and slammed her book closed. She slipped it into her bag, and left the room.

Outside, she paused. Yes, or no?

Nerves tingling in her stomach, Ella dug out her phone and pulled up James's number. She stared, debating, finger hovering over the call button.

Stop hiding.

She pressed the button, and walked off down the corridor as it dialled.

Time to stop hiding.

A FINAL REQUEST FOR MERCY

THE FULL MOON SHONE, BATHING THE YARD IN MUTED SILVER and turning Abbi into a dark, doggy shadow as she lay underneath the lemon tree. She stretched, tail thumping the ground; the night was warm, the Zac rabbit was home, and all was well with the world.

A movement caught her ear and she raised her muzzle to sniff. Algernon the guinea pig, appearing for a midnight snack in the cage across the yard. His head bobbed as he ate, ears flapping and lettuce crunch-crunching in his teeth.

The tip of Abbi's tail twitched. Chasing him around his cage never failed to amuse her—especially since he never failed to run.

Abbi sat up and scratched at her collar, which always managed to tickle the itchy spot under her chin. A good chase would help her forget the discomfort.

A soft moan made her ears prick high—but Algernon munched away as though nothing was wrong. Strange.

Abbi sauntered over to the hutch. "Hey, piggy-pig. What's up?"

Algernon ignored her, concentrating on his food.

Another moan.

Abbi's eyebrows twitched. "Zac?" she asked. "Is that you?" She lowered her head against the hutch, listening for the rabbit's presence. He mostly kept himself inside at nights, especially now the frosts were here—but moaning was new.

Another moan, and a rustle of straw. She pressed closer. "Zac?"

Zac's reply was so soft Abbi couldn't make out the words.

"Zac, is everything all right?"

Another faint response, almost beyond hearing. "Come here."

"I am here." She snuffed through the corner of the cage. "See?"

"Open... Open the lid."

Abbi started. "What?" she said. "It sounded like you said 'Open the lid'."

"Yes."

"What? No! I can't do that." She nodded towards the house. "They'd kill me."

"Please?"

"Why?"

"I... need you."

Abbi stared at the house, sleeping quietly in the night. She scratched at her ear, pondering. "I suppose so. If you really *need* me..."

"I do," Zac panted.

Abbi sighed. *Here goes nothing.* She leapt onto the roof of the cage where three bricks held down the lid. She shoved at one with her nose and it scraped a few centimetres. She shoved again and it toppled off, landing with a thunk. The other two followed, then she jumped back to the ground. She nibbled at the lid, trying to get a good grip.

"Please hurry."

Abbi tugged and the lid opened. She swallowed, half expecting one of the girls to burst out of the house and yell at her. But the house slept. She stuck her nose into the cage.

In the moonlight, the rabbit was nothing more than a silvery bump in a corner. Abbi twitched her nose; he smelled wrong. "Are you okay, Zac?"

The silvery mound shivered—Zac inched his head around to face her.

Abbi winced, sensing the effort that the simple movement took.

"No," he said in response to her question. "I'm not."

"What... what's wrong?"

Zac shuddered. "Die... dying."

Abbi jerked away. No. Zac had been sick, but that was before. He was better now. He couldn't be dying.

"Abbi?"

Her nose trembled. "I'm here."

"I... I want you to do me a favour."

"Zac, you're not dying, don't be silly. The girls will make you better, they fixed you last time—"

"No." His whisper was faint, so faint—but firm. Abbi shivered. "I didn't get better last time."

Abbi pawed at the ground. "What do you mean? You were running around like anything last week. They fixed you, the girls fixed you, they *did*."

Zac shook his head. "They didn't," he said. "Not forever. It's... it's come back, and this time... The vet couldn't help me. I can't beat it."

His head lolled against the straw and adrenalin flushed Abbi's system. "No, Zac!" His sides filled out again, and she breathed.

"I'm sorry," he said.

Abbi chest constricted, and she nudged him. "You can," she said. "Please, you can beat it." But the acrid scent of his illness crept into her nostrils, faint but inexorable, and deep inside she knew Zac was right.

"You smell it," he said, and she nodded. He drew a faltering breath. "I want you to end it."

Abbi leapt back, hackles raised, growling. "No! I won't do it."

Silence. Abbi crept back to the cage.

"Never... never mind." Zac flicked his vein-webbed ear, brushing it over Abbi's cheek.

She drew in a lungful of sick air, staring at him with misting eyes. Pain. She could smell it, all over him. He was right: he was dying.

"Just take me out," he said. "Let me... let me get out one last time."

She nudged him softly. "Okay."

For a moment she stood still, nose buried in the softness of his fur, feeling his heart beat against her and his breath shudder through his body. A queasy jolt ran through her stomach. "Zac, I can't do what you want. I can't."

Zac looked at her with somber eyes. "You will," he said. "When the time comes, you won't be able to stop yourself."

Abbi shifted, uneasy. "I'm sorry. I can't take you out of your cage after all. Not if that's what you want."

"Abbi, please. I... It hurts. I just want to feel the grass one last time."

She squeezed her eyes shut, but she couldn't block out the smell. She sighed. One quick run on the grass wouldn't hurt. Then she could just put him back in his cage, and everything would be fine.

Zac shuddered, whiskers tickling Abbi's nose.

She took him gently by the scruff of his neck.

Slowly, she eased him up, lifted him out of the cage, and placed him on the ground. She sat next to him and looked around the yard. The moonlight cast everything into relief, sharpening the edges, all black or silver.

Abbi glanced at Zac, shivering even though the night was warm. His fur glistened. She gave a half smile. Silver-furred rabbit and shadow-haired dog—together, they were the night.

She watched Zac out of the corner of her eye, wondering if perhaps he'd accepted her earlier response. Would he try to convince her? He sat with the air of someone waiting. But that might be nothing; he was probably working up the energy for one last tour of the yard.

And then, without warning, he leapt. Two feet up in the air, he bucked. He landed and sprinted down the yard, a silver blur in the half-light.

Abbi leapt to her feet in an instant, instinct in overdrive. It ran. *Chase. Chase!*

The blur was fast, but she was faster. *Chase! Catch!* She was the hunter and the prey would not escape.

Black paws flashed as she gained ground, step after step—and then she was on it. She reached it and teeth closed around fur, drew shut with a crunch. She lifted the furry mop and shook.

Prey. Caught it. She grinned, dropping the silver bundle on the ground. She sniffed at it, nudged it, bumped it, turned it over.

An eye caught the light.

Abbi's legs collapsed underneath her. "No," she said as she crumbled to the ground. "Zac!" She nuzzled the rabbit's soft stomach. "Zac-bunny, Zac, please, I'm sorry! I didn't mean it!"

But he didn't move.

She whimpered. "No." A howl rose in her throat and she lifted her nose to the sky. "Aroo! Arooooo!"

The neighbouring dogs took up her cry, sensing something amiss. Howls echoed through the night, a dirge, and a lament for what she had done.

It's his fault! she thought angrily. *He knew I'd chase if he ran! It's not my fault I'm a dog!* But the guilt still gnawed at her stomach.

Abbi rested her head on Zac's body. "I'm so sorry."

The body grew cold beneath her chin. She rose and lifted him in her mouth, gentle, as though he might break. She padded across the grass, slowly, deliberately, a funeral procession of one. She laid him back on the straw of the hutch and climbed in beside him. She curled up, her body shielding his, black and silver together in the black and silver night.

"Goodnight, Zac," she said, and wept.

LET US BE EXPLORERS

Let us
    hold hands together and head
    to places we have not been in forever
    that exist only in distant memories
    of having-been-there-once,
    of having-seen-that-then

Together, let us
    feast upon the honey that falls fresh from combs,
and
    travel south, to the springtime of
    the awakening bud, and then
    the strong branch that, laden,
    drips with new-pressed wine

Then let us
    climb the mountains of myrrh, and
    feast on pomegranates in the secret garden
    gently peel them open to suck
    at flesh pink, and pure, and delicious

Afterwards, let us stand
    before the tower of David

run fingers over satin sides of silk
caress the fawns that hide among the lilies, and
kiss the small pink seashells of our shores

Let us do these things
and let us do them slowly
for we are explorers
in no rush for anything
but the journey.

THE DAY THE DOG FIRST CALLED

THE DAY THE DOG FIRST CALLED, NATALIA HAD BEEN contemplating suicide. The cobwebby blackness that had once been confined to the upper corners of the house had recently begun to send out feelers and crisscross the ceiling, and she knew it wouldn't be too much longer before they reached down the walls and engulfed the floor, and then nowhere would be safe and she might as well be dead. Fear, however, held her back, and she was just contemplating her own futility when the doorbell rang.

Ordinarily, when the cobwebs pressed down and she couldn't breathe, Natalia ignored the doorbell—and the phone—but today, morbid as her thoughts were, she thought perhaps she might like to share them with someone. And so she answered the door.

"What do you think," she began, intending to question the visitor about means and methods, and stopped: the visitor was a shaggy, dirty-white dog. "Oh," Natalia finished instead. "I expect you don't think much about anything, do you."

The dog sat, pink tongue lolling to one side, and stared at her. "Well," it said. "I hope sometimes I do."

Natalia stared back. "I suppose you had better come in, then," she said at last. "Can't have you sit there all day."

The dog stood, and she motioned it into the house. It waited politely in the entryway for her to close the door, then followed her into the kitchen.

"Would you like a drink?" Natalia asked, moving stacks of dirty bowls onto piles of used plates. After all, a talking dog was no stranger than the cobwebs, and it never hurt to be polite. "Sorry about the mess."

"Not at all," replied the dog. "Some water would be lovely."

Natalia rummaged in the cupboards for something clean, settling at last on a greasy glass baking dish. Turning away, she gave it a quick polish with a tea towel that had seen better days and hoped the dog wouldn't mind. She filled it with cool water and set it on the floor.

"Thank you," the dog said, and lapped at it.

Natalia leaned back against the kitchen sink, watching the rhythmic motions of his mouth and overtly ignoring the black feeler that waved in her peripheral vision. Her husband had said ignoring her 'strange fantasies' might improve the situation, and while it had never worked yet, she felt she ought to at least make an effort in the presence of a guest.

The dog finished and raised his head, water dripping from his hairy chin. He glanced around and gestured at a second dirty tea towel lying crumpled on the floor. "May I?"

Natalia nodded. "Of course."

The dog padded over and wiped his chin before curling up on the floor at her feet and staring at the roof. "Dark in here, isn't it?" he said.

Natalia nodded again, her voice stuck behind the lump in her throat. She'd told her husband it was dark;

she told everyone that it was dark in here, that the cobwebs were growing, but all they did was look at her strangely and note how spotless the ceilings were. "Is it?" she asked the dog, quavering. "I hadn't noticed."

The dog twitched his eyebrow, managing to appear skeptical and sympathetic all at once. "I can help," he said. "If you like."

The lump in her throat melted into tears. "That... That would be nice."

He nodded, clambered to his feet, and bowed. "Good day, then," he said, and headed for the door.

Natalia's stomach leapt. "You're leaving?"

He smiled. "I'll come back."

Natalia sat cross-legged on the floor in the middle of the living room and wept. The cobwebs almost co-cooned her now, hovering a scant arm's length away no matter where she went. When her husband was home it was better; he still glowed like a flame in the dark, and the cobwebs shied away when he touched her. But he was impatient with what he called her theatrics, impatient at the growing pile of laundry and cupboards stripped bare to lay dirty offerings over stove and bench and sink.

"You could at least try something little," he'd said last night. "I'm sure it would make you feel better to accomplish something."

Probably, Natalia thought, he was right.

But moving through the cobwebs made her sick; the way they swayed and shifted in front of her, closing in behind, encircling and ensconcing and festooning her like she was a Christmas tree in need of stringing. And it had been a month since the dog had visited.

Fear hovered closer than the webs, stickier, more persistent. It stole the moisture from her mouth and slicked her hands with it instead, and whispered in her ear that things would never get better, that she would never be strong enough to burn away the webs the way her husband did, that she might as well die and save everyone the hassle.

Nodding vaguely, not quite certain what the hassle was but certain she was the cause, Natalia stood.

The webs circled and wavered before reforming closer than ever.

Natalia held a hand out in front of her and watched as tendrils of darkness darted in to lick at her fingers before melting away.

What would it be like, she wondered, to give in?

Superficially, she doubted the cobwebs would hurt her—their caresses seemed quite gentle—but instinctively she knew that they were like real webs, like spiders' webs, and that once she was in there would be no way out.

The doorbell rang, dispelling her line of thought.

Around her, the webs drew away.

Without cause, her heart began to pound. Perhaps she wanted to give in more than she liked to admit; perhaps she'd been looking forward to it, in a way, and now here was some stranger come to her door to interrupt her right at the pivotal moment.

Sighing, she went to the door and opened it. The shaggy dog sat patiently, a wooden box in his mouth.

"Oh," she greeted him again. "I'd given up on you coming back."

The dog nodded.

"Well, come in then." Natalia opened the door wide and allowed the dog in.

He trotted straight through to the living area with nary a glance at the cobwebs and sat in the middle of the room on the rug.

Natalia sat on the floor beside him. "So, what is your box?"

He placed it in her lap. "For you," he said gruffly. His gaze swept the room and he frowned. "I do hope you'll use it. This place has become positively gloomy."

And with that, he gave a flick of his tail and let himself out the front door, leaving Natalia wide-mouthed behind him, cradling the box.

She blinked. How bizarre.

She looked at the box in her hands, a rough, ugly-looking thing, all splintery and cracked.

Instinctively, she grabbed the top and tried to open it—but nothing happened. It seemed the box was just a solid cube of wood.

Anger welled in her chest and she gripped the box until her fingers hurt. What good was a horrible old box in times like these?

What was she supposed to do with it? Burn it, so the house might see a brief, ineffectual flash of light?

The tendrils of darkness closed around Natalia's wrists and she shook. How dare the dog abuse her hope like this, especially when it was so frail as to be almost non-existent?

The tendrils tightened, and she stared at them.

Yes, they were right.

Horrible old box. Why was she even holding it?

Abruptly, she stood and stalked to the bedroom, where she bent down and shoved the box under the bed, between musty blankets and a yellowed satin dress, to languish with the dust bunnies.

Natalia lay on her bed staring at nothing.

Well, she corrected herself, the darkness wasn't precisely nothing, but it might as well be.

Her husband muttered vaguely, something perhaps about the state of the house, or his mother, or a doctor, or something...

She didn't really care.

He'd been muttering for weeks, now, and she barely noticed anymore. The cobwebs smothered the sound, just like they smothered everything else—even feeling, even fear.

That was nice, the not-feeling-fear. It was nice to be able to go an entire day without seizing up in a panic, or shying away with heart pounding and mouth dry as a tendril of darkness brushed her shoulder.

They didn't brush her anymore, the cobwebs; they surrounded her.

It was the evening after the dog had come that last time that she'd given in and let herself be cocooned, and the cobwebby tendrils had led her to her bed and laid her down, and she'd only gotten up since to visit the bathroom—and sometimes even that seemed like too much effort.

But at least the fear was gone.

That was, that is, until a dog barked.

At first Natalia ignored it, much like she ignored everything that wasn't cobwebs and tendrils and darkness these days. Darkness was, after all, all-consuming.

But the dog continued, loud enough and long enough that the darkness grew irritated.

It shuddered and snapped, cracking against Natalia's wrists, and she winced away, separating herself from the dark by a tiny fraction for the first time in weeks.

The space was just big enough for the bark to fit into, and it filtered into Natalia's ears like poison, thick and cold like dread.

Her heart squeezed in on itself and her breath caught in her throat.

Desperately, she reached out for the darkness, but still the dog barked, and the darkness writhed away.

The space grew until the bark couldn't fill it, and fear seeped in. Natalia flailed in the sheets, ankles tangled, panic rising. "No," she whimpered. "No!"

Her breath came quickly and her heart raced, and the darkness swirled around, darting and flinching, trying to regain its hold on her. Natalia lifted up her hands, trying desperately to grasp the cobwebs, but the sheets pinned her down and the bark held her back, ringing in her head like a gong.

She thrashed sideways and slipped, fell between the bed and the wall, landed on the floor with a thud.

The air rushed out of her lungs and things fell silent: the barking ceased, the darkness stilled.

Natalia gasped for breath and squeezed her eyes closed. *What am I doing?* she thought. *What is happening to me? I don't want to be afraid.*

A faint memory of something more flickered in the dark, a feeling the dog had brought.

She moved to wrap her arms around herself and as she did her elbow bumped something solid and square.

She reached out for it and winced as a splinter snagged her fingertip. The box the dog had given her. Her breath hitched again in her throat.

Grasping the box against her, Natalia struggled out from behind the bed. Her hip bashed against the bedpost and she cried out.

The cobwebs shivered.

"No!" she cried. "Don't leave me."

They circled closer.

Natalia perched on the edge of the bed, cradling the box in her lap. What was it that the dog had said? "I hope you use it." Hope, that was it: that was what the dog had brought.

But how to use it?

She turned it over in her hands, searching the surface for a clue.

She frowned. Was that a hairline crack, blending with the grain of the wood? She worried it with her nail, hissing as wood jagged in tender skin.

There, it *was* a crack, she could see it clearly now.

The darkness swirled around her, whispering and fluttering—but she didn't notice.

Natalia wedged her nail in the crack and twisted. The nail chipped, but the lid of the box popped free and Natalia shied away instinctively.

Cautiously, through slitted eyes, Natalia peered into the box.

A large steel ring, a stiff, charred piece of cloth, and a chipped bit of flint lay inside. Natalia picked up the flint and struck it against the steel without pausing to think, because that was what they were for, and so that was what you did with them.

Sparks flew. The darkness howled.

Wide-eyed, Natalia stared at it. It twisted and writhed, and the howl was both pained and angry. She lifted a hand toward it, biting her lip. She didn't want to hurt the webs.

They'd kept her safe, protected her from fear...

What was it she'd been afraid of, though, exactly?

Living, maybe—but right now she couldn't quite remember what was so horrible about life, either. Natalia looked at the flint in her hand.

Use it, the dog had said. *It's dark in here.*

Surely it wouldn't hurt to try. Natalia struck the flint, and fire flared to life.

The darkness screeched and slapped her. Natalia gasped, grabbed at the sting on her cheek as tears sprang to her eyes.

This? This was what hope did, why the dog had told her to use the box? So she could anger the darkness, provoking it to hurt her? "I'm sorry!" she cried. "I didn't mean it!"

But she had: some tiny, desperate part of her had meant to light the flame and the darkness knew.

She wailed as it lashed out again, beating her. It twined tendrils through her hair and yanked, wound its way up her nose until she couldn't breathe, crushed her body in bands of black so tight her ribs cracked.

Natalia tried to thrash, tried to escape, but the darkness held her tight and she couldn't even scream.

The flint cut into her fingers and, desperation slicing through the fear, she struck again, again, again. "Stop! Please, just stop!"

The darkness roared, thrashed at her once more—and withdrew.

When Natalia opened her eyes, the darkness hung in the corners of the ceiling like cobwebs—like it had so many months ago when the dog had first come to call.

She stared at it, breath held, waiting for it to lunge—but it stayed.

Slowly, she released her breath.

Natalia looked at the box near her feet, the steel and flint in her hands. The darkness wasn't gone—but now it would live in her house on her terms.

THE REMARKABLE INSIGHT OF JELLYBEANS

THEY SIT ON THE LOUNGE THEY BOUGHT TOGETHER, CURLED up in opposite ends while the TV blares. He sounds like the TV, droning on, talking with monotonous fervour about his job, his friends, his bike—and she can't make herself care. It's like ads, like prime time, like seeing the same reruns month after month after month, and what was clever and funny once is now mundane. It makes her think of canned laughter and dishes, taking out the garbage and catching buses. Forever, it's been like this; he talks, she listens, never interrupting, never inter-jecting, the perfect girlfriend, the perfect listener, per-fectly selfless, an empty vessel just waiting to be filled —and he's never asked about her day, not once.

He pauses for a breath and, carefully, she lifts the jellybean jar from where it has been resting against her tucked-up ankles, out of sight but not out of mind, cool glass pressing against bare skin, ice in a beige desert storm. She unscrews it with perfect, measured move-ments, not too quick, not too loud, not wanting to interrupt his train of thought.

He glances over. "Can I have some?"

He hadn't wanted her to buy them, called them a frivolous waste of money, and as soon as she got them home she felt like he was right; jellybeans had no place in their pantry, nowhere to sit that didn't highlight their out-of-placeness, garish in the cool dim company of potatoes and garlic, practical tinned tomatoes and stockpiles of penne pasta. He hadn't wanted her to buy them, but she'd known all along he'd finish most of them, because that's just how it was, and she'd never interrupted.

"Sure." She peers down at a jar full of sugar, bright colour and empty calories, flavour that kisses the tongue then vanishes, leaving the mouth cloyed with generic sweetness. Bright colours, like fruit, or hummingbirds, or hope.

She chooses a dark brown one speckled with white, then twists around, arm extended so she can pop it into his mouth, a sugar pill, a placebo. His tongue brushes her fingertips, bird-like, here-and-then-gone, and she returns her fingers to her lap and rubs them on her skirt.

"Yuck," he says, screwing up his nose, eyes never leaving the TV. "I hate the coffee ones."

"Sorry," she says, and fishes a second bean from the jar, brown, with white speckles. "Another?"

He nods, and stares glazedly at the telly; he has exhausted his supply of conversation topics, and she is unsurprised, because every night they are the same, and they are limited, and they are never hers, like the books kept on display to impress the neighbours or the ornaments that line the hallway. She presses the jellybean against his lips, a tiny act of rebellion, and he takes it without looking, and again she scrubs her fingers on her skirt.

He makes a face and spits out something that was perfect once, but is now half-chewed and mangled, its clear, worthless centre exposed: a shot of glucose, an empty hope, a painted, hollow corpse. "I just said I don't like the coffee ones," he snaps, shooting a sideways glare into her temple where it pierces, lodges, and she can almost feel the blood trickling down.

"Sorry!" she says defensively, resisting the need to rub her temple. "I didn't mean it." But a thrill stirs inside her stomach. He'll believe her, of course he will, because she never interrupts—but this time, she meant it, and she hears alarums sound and horses neigh, and the clash of sword on shield.

"Hmph." He reaches into the jar and scoops out his own handful, multi-coloured like the eggs of a rainbow, then scoffs them down all at once, chewing indiscriminately.

What's the point? she wonders. Why have different flavours in the first place, if you won't stop to savour them?

She closes her eyes and selects one bean, just one, its sugary surface smooth and slightly sticky. Without opening her eyes, she places it delicately on her tongue, closes her mouth around it like a secret, sucks it close and concentrates. Sharp, sweet but acid, tart—not lemon, but something close.

Grapefruit, she decides, and rolls it between her teeth, trying to make the flavour last—but of course, the flavour's gone and she's left with that same inevitable, generic sweetness.

She feels the same; just a generic sort of sweet, a hollow-caloried person-shaped lump, valueless, worthless but for fleeting gratification that weighs heavy afterwards on the tongue. Does he feel that way about her? Although she listens, does it satisfy him? After the first flavour of their relationship is gone, is she still enough?

She watches as he grabs another handful of jelly-beans and sucks them down, swallowing them like liquid, concentration on the sitcom never faltering. Yes. He is satisfied with bright colours that smack of hope. Empty nutrients comfort him.

She remembers the man she saw earlier this evening, dark and tall, striding between the rows of the fruit market with confidence like a million-dollar cruiser amidst dinghies. He'd confronted a seller over her bruised nectarines, their blushing skins marred by brown stains of abuse. He'd caressed ripe lady fingers, inhaled sour green mangoes, savoured a dark burgundy grape. Not everyone is satisfied by hollowness, she realises.

She is not satisfied.

He shifts beside her, mindless, and she knows that any moment now he will ask for his nightly cup of coffee—supermarket coffee, over-roasted coffee, old and dull and cheap coffee. But she is sick of crappy coffee; it reminds her of days spent under the flickering eye of fluorescent light bulbs, walled in by partitions covered with geometric patterns in sensible colours meant to detract from the fact that really, they are padded.

A shiver touches her spine and she stares at the jellybeans, wondering.

And of course, "Coffee?" he says, and she wraps her fingers around the neck of the jar and decides. Generic sweetness is not inevitable. "No," she says as her heart tries to break open her rib cage, or burst her veins with blood flow. She touches her fingertips to her temple.

He tears himself away from cued laughter and crude humour to give her an incredulous stare. "What do you mean?"

She shakes her head, lips sealed against the weight of what she has said. She can't repeat it, it's too heavy, it will break her jaw with its passing—but she has said it once, and maybe once will be enough.

He raises an eyebrow. "Bad day at work?"

And there it is, the very thing she's been waiting for all these months, the thing she thought she needed to hear—only now, she realises it's not enough. It's jelly-beans, with the gloss of hope hiding emptiness inside, and he, who is satisfied with handfuls of sugar and cheap, dirty coffee, will never be enough.

She thinks again of the man in the markets, of sun-ripened strawberries made sweet with heat, of apples crisp and fresh so the juice runs down her chin when she bites into them, and she turns to him with eyes full of tears, with hands full of jellybeans, and a heart full of fruit. "I'm sorry," she says, and catches his arm before he can turn away, before he can dismiss her words as platitudes. "I can't stay here," she whispers, begging him to understand and knowing perfectly well that candy and cost-saving never can. "I'm leaving. I'm sorry," and she's not.

While he sits there in stunned silence, she passes him the jellybean jar and stands. "You'll be fine," she says, and smiles. "What we have is replaceable."

Gaping, he watches as she walks to the bedroom, where she picks up her blackwood jewellery box that holds the antique necklace she asked her grandma for when she was twelve, empties the single drawer in the dresser that holds all the clothes she's ever chosen for herself, slips on her favourite shoes and rummages in the depths of the wardrobe for the pale blue, fake-crocodile handbag she'd fallen in love with at the county show, the one he hated so much she'd never dared use. It smells of feet and old carpet, pencils and overripe bananas. A smile spreads across her face as she gathers up all the decisions she's ever made, and carries them to her car.

"I'm sorry," she says as he stands on the porch, still speechless.

But she's not, and she drives away with the satisfying sweetness of mangoes on her tongue.

ABOUT THE AUTHOR

AMY LAURENS is an Australian author of fantasy fiction for all ages. Her story *Bones Of The Sea*, about creepy carnivorous mist and bone curses, won the 2021 Aurealis Award for Best Fantasy Novella.

Amy has also written the award-winning portal-fantasy *Sanctuary* series about Edge, a 13-year-old girl forced to move to a small country town because of witness protection (the first book is *Where Shadows Rise*), the humorous fantasy *Kaditeos* series, following newly graduated Evil Overlord Mercury as she attempts to acquire a castle, the young adult series *Storm Foxes*, about love and magic and family in small town Australia, and a whole host of non-fiction.

Head to www.AmyLaurens.com to find out more!

Read more by Amy Laurens!

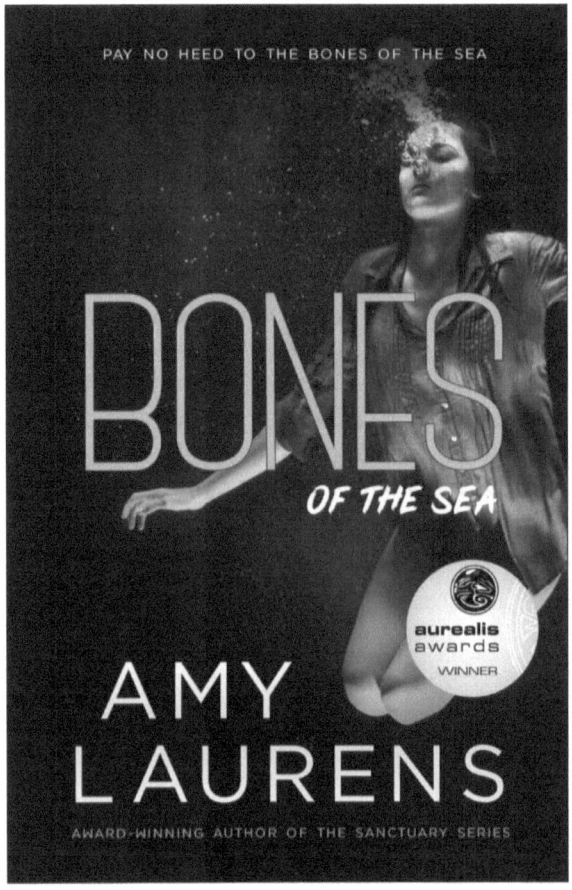

FOR A
Little While

A COLLECTION OF POEMS

AMY LAURENS

poems of becoming

CHANGE
BECOMES US

AMY LAURENS

Aurealis Award-winning author